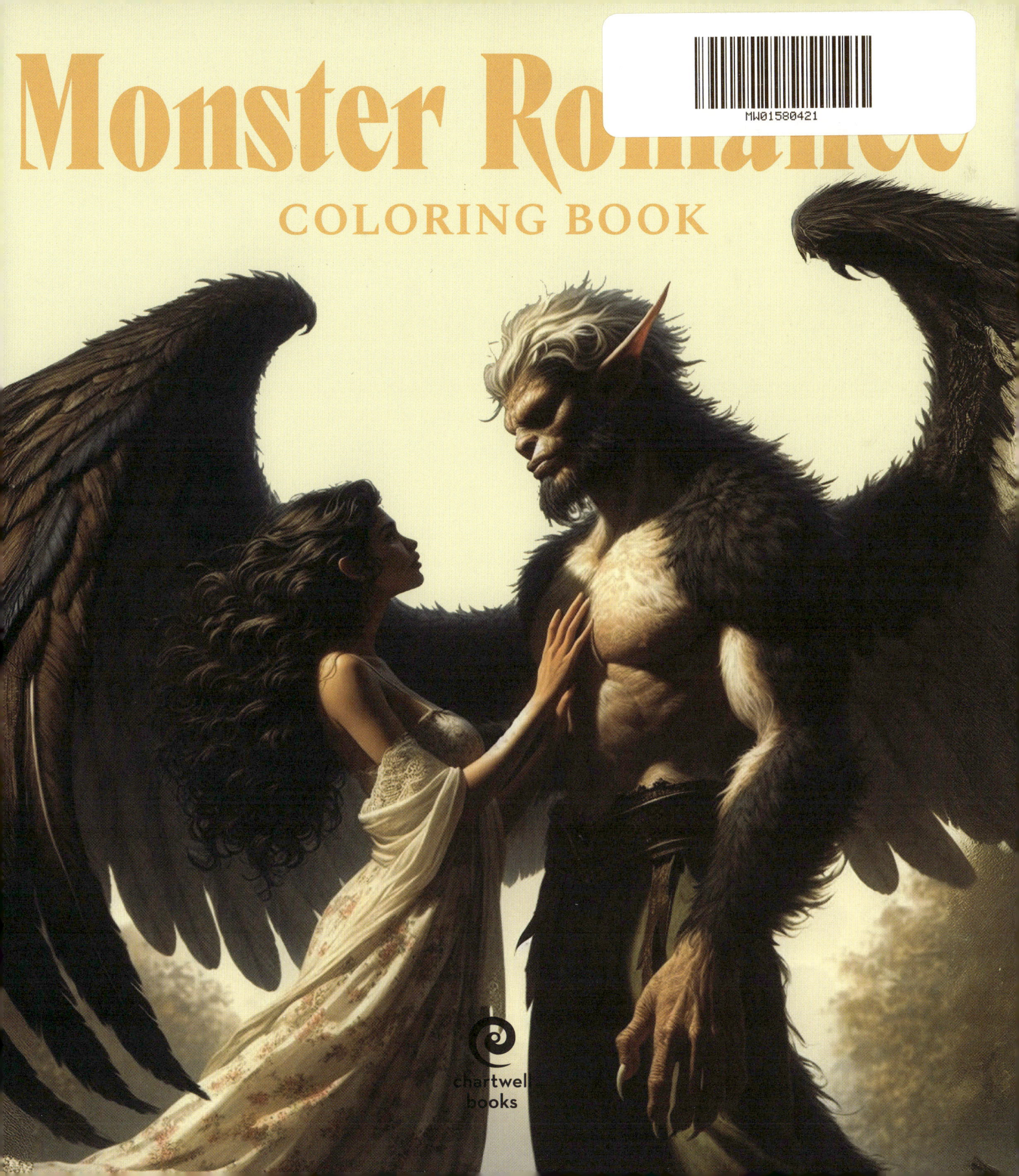

Find Beauty in the Unusual, the Unconventional, and the Forbidden!

Monster romance is the hottest new literary subgenre. It blends elements of fantasy, horror, and romance and readers can't get enough! It draws inspiration from ancient mythology, classical literature, and gothic fiction, to create a thriving genre in modern fiction and popular culture.

Readers are attracted to monster romance because it offers a unique blend of romance, fantasy, and exploration of themes that go beyond the boundaries of traditional love stories. As the name suggests, in these novels, the human heroine falls in love with a monster. And unlike vampire stories, these monsters cannot pass as human. They range from minotaurs, demons, mermen, aliens, kraken, and even cryptids like the mothman.

These tales provide an opportunity to experience a different kind of romance and engage with themes of love, acceptance, and personal growth in extraordinary and imaginative settings. Monster romance stories often explore themes of forbidden love, overcoming societal prejudices, and finding beauty in the unconventional.

And while this latest wave of novels has taken the genre to new levels, there are examples of monster romance throughout both historical literature, fairytales, and legends. Tales like *Beauty and the Beast, King Kong,* and numerous classical myths are all early examples of the genre.

Fans of monster romance will love the fun, "safe for work" romantic scenes to color. Let your imagination run wild! No artistic talent required, just a desire to escape to the mundane and travel to a world where love conquers all.

Quarto

© 2025 Quarto Publishing Group USA Inc.

This edition published in 2025 by Chartwell Books,
an imprint of The Quarto Group
142 West 36th Street, 4th Floor
New York, NY 10018 USA
T (212) 779-4972 F (212) 779-6058
www.Quarto.com

All rights reserved. No part of this book may be reproduced in any form without written permission of the copyright owners. All images in this book have been reproduced with the knowledge and prior consent of the artists concerned, and no responsibility is accepted by producer, publisher, or printer for any infringement of copyright or otherwise, arising from the contents of this publication. Every effort has been made to ensure that credits accurately comply with information supplied. We apologize for any inaccuracies that may have occurred and will resolve inaccurate or missing information in a subsequent reprinting of the book.

10 9 8 7 6 5 4 3 2 1

Chartwell titles are also available at discount for retail, wholesale, promotional, and bulk purchase. For details, contact the Special Sales Manager by email at specialsales@quarto.com or by mail at The Quarto Group, Attn: Special Sales Manager, 100 Cummings Center Suite 265D, Beverly, MA 01915, USA.

ISBN: 978-0-7858-4671-0

Publisher: Wendy Friedman
Publishing Director: Meredith Mennitt
Designer: Alana Ward
Editor: Meredith Mennitt
Image credits: Shutterstock

Printed in China